D0029093

For the sparkling Carrie Morling,
with love

Special thanks to
Sue Mongredien

ORCHARD BOOKS
338 Euston Road, London NW1 3BH
Orchard Books Australia
Level 17/207 Kent Street, Sydney, NSW 2000
A Paperback Original

First published in 2007 by Orchard Books
Rainbow Magic is a registered trademark of Working Partners Limited.
Series created by Working Partners Limited, London W6 OQT

Text © Working Partners Limited 2007
Cover illustrations © Georgie Ripper 2007
Inside illustrations © Orchard Books 2007

A CIP catalogue record for this book is available
from the British Library.

ISBN 978 1 84616 458 3
1 3 5 7 9 10 8 6 4 2

Printed in Great Britain

Orchard Books is a division of Hachette Children's Books

www.orchardbooks.co.uk

Pippa the Poppy Fairy

by Daisy Meadows

ORCHARD BOOKS

www.rainbowmagic.co.uk

The Fairyland Palace
Blossom Hall
Fairy Garden
Leafley Village
Visitors' Centre

Jack Frost's
Ice Castle
ossom Lake
Picnic Spot
The Park
Petal Perfection
Flower Shop
Blossom Village
High St
Rainbow Falls Gardens
Chaney Court Flower Show

I need the magic petals' powers,
To give my castle garden flowers.
And so I use my magic well
To work against the fairies' spell.

From my wand ice magic flies,
Frosty bolt through fairy skies.
And this crafty spell I weave
To bring the petals back to me.

Contents

Special Delivery	9
A Window Seat	21
Goblins Get a Ride	31
Petal Pandemonium	43
Ice Magic	55
Petal Perfection	67

"I love Blossom Hall!" Kirsty Tate sighed happily, as she finished off a delicious bowl of fruit and cereal.

She was sitting on the sunny terrace of the hotel restaurant with her best friend Rachel Walker and their parents. The two families were spending a week at the old Tudor house which was now a hotel, over the Easter holidays. The sky was blue, and the pink and white cherry trees in the gardens were in full bloom.

"It's lovely," Rachel agreed.

"Did you find the Fairy Garden yesterday?" Mrs Tate asked.

Rachel and Kirsty nodded.

"It was magic!" Rachel said, and she and Kirsty grinned at each other.

The two girls shared a very special secret. On a previous holiday they had become friends with the fairies. Yesterday, in the hotel garden, they had met Tia the Tulip Fairy, and begun a whole new fairy adventure.

"What do you two want to do today?" asked Mr Walker.

"We'd like to explore inside Blossom Hall this morning," Rachel said eagerly.

"I can't wait to look around," Kirsty added. "Mum, please can we—"

"Yes, you can leave the table if you've finished," Mrs Tate laughed.

"All the more bacon and eggs for me!" Mr Walker said teasingly as the girls got up.

Laughing, Rachel and Kirsty left the restaurant and set off down one of the winding corridors, looking at the pictures on the walls.

One of them showed a pretty village green. "That's Blossom Village, isn't it?" Kirsty said.

Rachel nodded. They had driven through the village to reach Blossom Hall.

"This is Blossom Hall," Rachel remarked, pausing in front of another print. "It says it was built in 1550!"

Next to the picture of Blossom Hall hung an oil painting of a field scattered with wildflowers: scarlet poppies, golden buttercups and blue cornflowers.

"It's lucky they're only painted flowers," Rachel sighed, "or they'd all be dying now that the Petal Fairies' magic petals have been stolen!"

The girls had learned that Jack Frost was causing trouble for the fairies. He had sent his goblin servants to steal the seven magic petals and, without them, flowers in Fairyland and in the human world couldn't bloom properly. The Petal Fairies had tried to get their petals back, but in the struggle between their magic and Jack Frost's icy spell, the petals had spun out of sight into the human world. Jack Frost had sent his goblins to bring them back, but Rachel and Kirsty were determined to find them first and return them to Fairyland.

"At least we managed to find Tia's Tulip Petal yesterday," Kirsty said. "I wonder if we'll find another magic petal today."

"I hope so," Rachel replied.

The girls arrived at the hotel reception, a spacious hallway with stained glass windows and a large mahogany table with a display of flowers. At that moment the main doors opened and a man in blue overalls came in, carrying an enormous basket of flowers.

"Hello, Bill," said Jenny, the receptionist. "Can you put the flowers in their usual place, please?"

Bill went over to the table, removed the old basket of dying flowers and put the new one in its place. Rachel thought the flowers were beautiful, especially the huge poppies. Their silky petals were gorgeous rich shades of red and orange, which contrasted with their jet-black centres.

Bill went over to the reception desk, and began to discuss next week's order with Jenny. Rachel and Kirsty could see that he had Petal Perfection Flower Shop printed on the back of his overalls.

"That's the flower shop in Blossom Village," Kirsty said to Rachel. "We drove past it on our way here."

"We'll do our best, Jenny," Bill was saying, "but we're having a lot of problems at the moment. Our flowers are dying very quickly and we don't know why!"

Kirsty sighed. "It's because six of the seven magic petals are still missing," she whispered to Rachel. "New flowers won't grow, and the ones which have already bloomed don't last very long at all."

Rachel nodded sadly in agreement.

Bill took out his notebook. "I'll go and get the rest of the order from the hotel manager," he said, and hurried off.

Rachel stared at the flowers Bill had just brought in. She could see that some of them were already wilting even though they were fresh from the flower shop. Suddenly her heart skipped a beat. "Kirsty," she whispered, clutching her friend's arm, "I just saw some red fairy sparkles shoot out of the basket!"

"Oh!" Kirsty looked thrilled.

The two girls hurried over to the flowers. As they reached them, there was another shower of crimson sparkles, and a tiny fairy zoomed out from the middle of a scarlet poppy.

"Oh, girls, I am glad to see you!" Pippa the Poppy Fairy exclaimed, dancing through the air towards Kirsty and Rachel. She wore a floaty scarlet dress, a matching hairband and tiny ballet shoes decorated with poppies.

"Hello, Pippa," Kirsty said excitedly. "Do you think your magic petal's here?"

Pippa's glittering wings drooped a little. "No, it's not here," she said sadly. "But I know where it is!" "Tell us, Pippa," Rachel urged. "Well, I was in the flower shop in Blossom Village, looking for my petal," Pippa explained. "But I was so busy looking that I got swept up in this basket of flowers and carried out of the shop!"

"So that's how you arrived here," said Kirsty.

Pippa nodded. "And I'm glad you and Rachel found me," she added, "because I didn't know where I was going to end up. But I'm sure I saw my magic petal just as I got carried out of the shop, so I must get back there as quickly as possible!"

Kirsty and Rachel glanced round cautiously. The reception area was getting very busy as people passed through on their way to and from breakfast.

"Let's go over to the window seat and think of a plan," Rachel suggested.

Pippa nodded and dived into Rachel's pocket as the girls hurried over to the large bay window and sat down on the velvet cushions.

"Look at my poor poppies," Pippa said, peeping out and pointing at the basket of flowers. Rachel and Kirsty could see that the delicate flowerheads were already starting to droop.

"I must get my magic petal back so that the poppies, and the other red flowers – which are all controlled by the Poppy Petal – can grow beautifully again!"

"The tulips are lovely," Kirsty remarked, gazing at the orange flowers which were blooming brightly. "That's because we found Tia the Tulip Fairy's petal yesterday."

Pippa nodded. "But only when we have all the magic petals safely back in Fairyland, will all the flowers in the human world be able to grow properly again," she pointed out.

"We'll find them," Rachel said in a determined voice.

"Don't forget that the goblins have a wand full of Jack Frost's icy magic to help them," Pippa said with a shiver. "We must be careful, girls."

Kirsty nodded, but just then a movement outside the window caught her eye. She turned to look. There, to her dismay, was a big, green goblin running at full speed across the hotel courtyard.

"Look, it's a goblin!" Kirsty gasped.

The goblin was running towards a white van parked outside the hotel. Petal Perfection Flower Shop was painted on the side of the van in curly green letters, and its back doors were wide open. As the girls and Pippa watched, the goblin skidded to a halt and waved his arms. Immediately a whole band of goblins raced out of the shrubbery. One of them was carrying the glittering icy wand which Jack Frost had given them.

"There are lots of them!" Pippa whispered anxiously as the goblins began climbing onto each other's shoulders to get inside the van.

"They're looking for the magic petal," Rachel replied.

Pippa shook her head. "It was left behind in the shop; I'm sure of it," she said.

"Look at what the goblins are doing now!" Kirsty remarked, frowning.

All the goblins had climbed inside the delivery van. The girls and Pippa couldn't see them, but what they could see were flowers flying out of the open doors of the van. Daffodils, tulips and other flowers came hurtling out, landing in a heap in the courtyard.

"Oh!" Pippa cried, clasping her hands together in horror. "How can they treat those beautiful flowers like that? We must stop them!"

"Yes, and quickly, too," Rachel added anxiously. "Before the delivery man sees them!"

Goblins Get a Ride

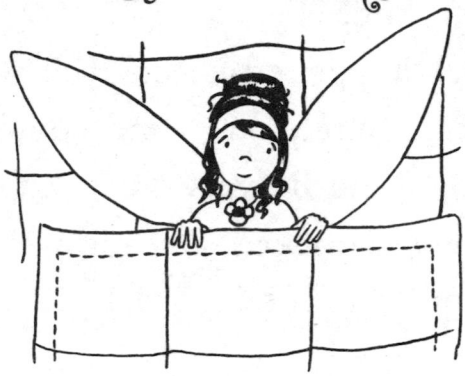

Quickly Pippa nestled down inside Rachel's pocket again, and the two girls jumped up. But they were too late! Bill was already at the hotel door, waving goodbye to Jenny.

"I'll take your order straight back to the shop," he was saying. "Goodbye."

Kirsty and Rachel glanced at each

other in dismay as Bill went out. They rushed after him into the courtyard and were just in time to see him picking up the flowers which were scattered on the ground.

"What's happened here?" Bill was muttering. "Surely the wind couldn't have blown the flowers out of my van. I must have knocked some flowers over when I got the hotel's order out."

The girls watched as Bill carefully loaded the flowers back into the van and then closed the doors. They couldn't see a single goblin though.

"Do you think the goblins jumped out before Bill got there?" whispered Rachel.

"I don't know," Kirsty said, frowning.

Bill jumped into the van and, with a cheery wave at the girls, he drove off.

"Kirsty!" Rachel cried suddenly. "Look at the back of the van!"

Kirsty's heart sank. There, grinning at them from the back windows of the van, were the goblins! They were pulling faces at Pippa and the girls, sticking their tongues out and waggling their fingers behind their ears. As the van pulled away, they waved a cheeky goodbye, looking very pleased with themselves.

"The goblins are on their way to the flower shop," Rachel groaned.

"They might even find Pippa's magic petal!" added Kirsty.

"And I don't even want to think about all the damage those naughty goblins could do in the flower shop," Pippa said. "Girls, we must go after them!"

"I'm sure our parents will let us go to the village," said Kirsty. "It's only at the end of the hotel drive."

"But we'll need a reason to go to the flower shop," Rachel pointed out.

Kirsty nodded thoughtfully, but at that moment she noticed a crumpled piece of paper lying on the gravel driveway. She picked it up.

"What's that?" asked Rachel curiously.

Kirsty smoothed the paper flat. Across the top, the words "Petal Perfection Flower Shop, High Street, Blossom Village" were printed. There was some writing underneath.

"One basket of pink roses, one bouquet of pink and white tulips," Kirsty read out. "This is the hotel's order for next week. Bill must have dropped it."

"Perfect!" Rachel beamed happily. "We can go into the flower shop to return it."

Pippa was so excited, she twirled herself out of Rachel's pocket in a shower of red sparkles. "Hurry, girls!" she said eagerly. "You'd better go and ask your parents' permission."

"I'll do that," Rachel replied. "Maybe we could borrow some of the hotel bikes, Kirsty. The driveway's really long, and it would be much quicker than walking."

"Good idea," Kirsty agreed. The girls knew that Blossom Hall kept bicycles for guests to use to explore the countryside. "I'll ask Jenny."

"I'll wait here," Pippa said, zooming out of sight behind a nearby shrub.

Rachel hurried off to find their parents while Kirsty went back into reception.

"Of course you can borrow some bikes, Kirsty," Jenny said kindly. "Come with me."

The receptionist took Kirsty to a large garage behind the hotel where the bikes were stored. She gave Kirsty padlocks and chains for the bikes, and two safety helmets. Then she helped Kirsty wheel the bikes round to the hotel driveway, before returning to the reception desk.

"That was quick!" Pippa whispered, popping out of the shrubbery as soon as Jenny had disappeared.

"And here comes Rachel," said Kirsty.

"We can go," Rachel announced, "but we can't leave the village and we must be back in an hour."

Pippa immediately flew into the basket on the front of Rachel's bike and settled herself comfortably inside. "Let's go," she cried. "We haven't a moment to lose!"

The girls put on their helmets, climbed onto the bikes and pedalled off as fast as they could go. It was a very long and winding driveway, and soon they were panting hard.

"Look at the hedgerows," Pippa pointed out, as the gates at the end of the drive finally came into sight. "Even my beautiful wild poppies are dying!"

Rachel and Kirsty could see that the scarlet poppies were indeed wilting. Not only that, but many of the primroses and cowslips in the hedgerows were dying too, even though they were supposed to be in full bloom.

"We must get all the magic petals back," said Rachel in a determined voice, forcing herself to pedal faster.

Petal Perfection Flower Shop was in the high street near the village green.

"Let's hope the goblins haven't found my magic petal yet," Pippa whispered, as she slipped into Rachel's pocket.

Kirsty and Rachel locked up their bikes, took off their helmets and hurried into the shop. There was nobody inside except a woman with long dark hair tied up in a ponytail. She was standing behind the counter, frowning, as she put blue irises and yellow roses together in a beautiful arrangement.

"Oh, dear!" the woman sighed as she laid aside a drooping rose. Then she spotted Rachel and Kirsty. "Hello," she said, looking flustered. "Sorry, I didn't see you there. I'm having such problems with my flowers."

Rachel and Kirsty glanced around the shop. They could see that many of the flowers on display in tall silver vases were looking sad and bedraggled. The poppies were especially bad, their large heads drooping and their fragile petals brown at the edges.

"We've got lots of orders to fill. I don't know how I'm going to manage," the woman went on. "Anyway, I'm Kate. My husband, Bill, and I own the shop. What can I do for you?"

"We're staying at Blossom Hall," Kirsty explained, holding out the piece of paper. "Bill came this morning with the flowers, but he accidentally dropped next week's order when he left."

Kate beamed at them. "Oh, thank you, girls," she said gratefully. "Bill got back a little while ago, but he's just popped out in the van to deliver another order."

Rachel and Kirsty glanced at each other, wondering if the goblins had managed to escape from the van and get into the shop.

"I must finish this bouquet for a new mum," Kate explained. "But why don't you pop through to the back room and choose some flowers to take home with you as a thank you?"

"Yes, please," Rachel and Kirsty chorused.

Kate pointed at a door behind the counter. "It's through there," she said. "Just help yourselves."

"Perfect!" Pippa whispered, popping her head out of Rachel's pocket as soon as they had closed the door behind them. "Now we'll have a chance to look for my magic petal!"

"And maybe the goblins, too," added Kirsty.

Quickly the girls and Pippa hurried into the back room.

"Oh, no," Rachel groaned, coming to a halt in the doorway. "The goblins are here!"

The goblins were running around, frantically looking for the magic petal, and the room was a complete mess. Pippa and the girls stared in dismay at the buckets of flowers that had been kicked over, and at the floor awash with water. There were stray petals and leaves everywhere.

But the goblins were having great fun! One had got himself wrapped in a roll of pink, flowery wrapping paper. He looked like an Egyptian mummy, with just his big green ears, nose and feet sticking out. Another had draped himself in multi-coloured ribbons and was swinging another long ribbon over his head like a lasso. The goblin with the wand had a large daffodil stuck behind each ear and a garland of daisies round his neck.

"I don't think they've found the petal yet," Kirsty whispered. She, Rachel and Pippa couldn't help laughing at the goblins' antics, even though they were horrified by the mess.

"No, they're having too much fun!" Rachel replied. "Look, one's got stuck!"

The biggest goblin was upside-down in an empty flower bucket, his legs waving in the air. He was yelling loudly, but his voice was muffled, so nobody could hear what he was saying.

Pippa and the girls watched as two other goblins grabbed his legs and yanked him out.

As his head came out of the bucket, the girls could see that he was grinning. "I've found the magic petal!" he shouted triumphantly.

Rachel, Kirsty and Pippa stared in horror as the goblin held up a beautiful scarlet poppy petal.

"I'm going to take it straight to Jack Frost!" he boasted.

"No, I want to!" one of the others yelled. All the other goblins immediately joined in, trying to grab the fragile petal.

Rachel couldn't bear to see the petal in danger of being ripped apart. "Give that back!" she demanded bravely. The goblins all turned to glare at her.

"Shan't!" the biggest goblin sneered. He dashed out of the back door of the shop, immediately followed by all the other goblins.

"We can't follow them or Kate will wonder where we've gone," Rachel said. "We'd better go out the front way."

"Can you clean up this mess, Pippa?" asked Kirsty.

Quickly Pippa waved her wand and a shower of fairy sparkles magically cleared up the whole room, rolling up the wrapping paper and ribbons and putting the flowers back into their buckets.

"I can't make the wilting flowers bloom properly, though, without my magic petal," Pippa sighed, whizzing into Rachel's pocket.

The two girls raced back into the shop.

Kate looked at them in surprise.

"Didn't you find any flowers you liked?" she asked.

"We, er, just remembered something we have to do in the village first," Kirsty stammered.

"We'll come back later to collect some flowers, if that's OK," added Rachel.

"That's fine," Kate replied.

Quickly the girls unlocked their bikes and pedalled round to the back of the store. "There they go!" Rachel shouted, catching a glimpse of the goblins running into the park.

The girls pedalled after them. But by the time they had cycled into the park, the goblins were nowhere to be seen.

"They must be here somewhere," Kirsty said. She gazed around as they came to a halt underneath an oak tree. She could see trees and flowerbeds, and a hill nearby, but no goblins.

Ssshhh!

The sound came from above, startling Kirsty. She glanced up and saw a very odd-looking green branch. Kirsty clapped a hand to her mouth as she realised it was a goblin's leg!

As quietly as she could, she got off her bike, tapped Rachel on the shoulder and pointed upwards. Rachel and Pippa saw the leg and Pippa nodded as Rachel climbed off her bike.

"We'll fly up there and try to grab the petal," Pippa whispered, waving her wand.

Rachel and Kirsty felt a rush of excitement as a cloud of crimson sparkles instantly transformed them into fairies. Silently fluttering their glittering wings, the three friends flew up into the branches of the tree.

"There!" Pippa said softly, pointing with her wand.

The goblins were sitting in a long line on a sturdy branch, their legs dangling. The biggest goblin was at the end, holding the magic petal.

Rachel, who was closest, immediately flew down and made a grab for it. But at the last moment the goblin saw her coming and batted her away.

"It's those pesky girls again!" he called furiously. "Do something!"

"I'll cast a really brilliant spell," yelled the goblin with the wand. "Er, um..."

"Get on with it!" shouted the biggest goblin as Pippa, Rachel and Kirsty hovered around him, trying to grab the petal.

"OK, I've got it," replied the goblin

with the wand. "To escape these girls would be quite nice—" he began, shaking the wand.

"Nice!" shouted the biggest goblin angrily. "It would be brilliant! Not nice!"

"I don't know any words that rhyme with 'brilliant'!" the goblin with the wand said sulkily, and Pippa and the girls laughed.

"To escape these girls would be quite nice," the goblin said again, pointing the wand at the ground. "I demand an icy slide. I mean – a slide of ice!" he finished.

Immediately a huge chute of ice appeared, running from the branches of the tree to the grass below. One by one the goblins leapt on to it with gleeful shrieks and slid to the ground. The biggest goblin took one last swipe at Pippa and the girls and

then followed his friends down the slide.

"They're escaping with the magic petal!" Kirsty cried in dismay as the goblins dashed away.

Pippa and the girls flew down from the tree as the goblins fled up the nearby hill. With a deft flick of her wand, Pippa made Rachel and Kirsty human-sized again, and the girls jumped on their bikes.

"After them!" Rachel cried.

The girls zoomed off after the goblins,

Pippa riding in the basket on the front of Rachel's bike. They reached the foot of the hill really quickly, but then they began to struggle.

"It's hard pedalling uphill!" Kirsty panted, straining to go faster.

Pippa leaned out of the basket and waved her wand. Dazzling poppy-red sparkles swirled down onto both bikes' wheels.

"Oh," Rachel yelled happily, "I'm going much faster now!"

"Me, too," Kirsty agreed. "Thanks, Pippa."

With the help of fairy magic, the girls started gaining on the goblins.

"We're going to overtake the goblins soon," called Rachel.

"Let's try to grab the petal as we pass them," Kirsty suggested.

"Look, the goblin with the petal is a little behind the others," Pippa pointed out.

"Kirsty, I'll ride past on his right-hand side, and you ride past on his left," Rachel said. "Then he can't escape."

"Good plan," Kirsty agreed.

As the two girls came up behind the goblin, Rachel went right and Kirsty went left. The goblin was clutching the petal in his right hand, and Rachel reached out for it as she rode up behind him.

But at the last moment the goblin spotted her. "Trying to trick me, are you?" he jeered. "You'll have to try harder than that!" And, laughing gleefully, he quickly transferred the petal from his right hand to his left.

But at that very moment, Kirsty sailed past the goblin on his other side, and she reached out and grabbed the petal from his hand while the goblin was still laughing at Rachel.

"Hurrah!" Pippa cried, as they raced on past the other goblins.

"Hey!" shouted the big goblin angrily. "Give that magic petal back!"

The other goblins had now realised what had happened, but they were too late.

Rachel and Kirsty were speeding away on their bikes. Behind them, they could hear the goblins shouting and arguing with each other because they'd lost the magic petal.

"Girls, I can never thank you enough," Pippa announced as they finally came full circle and arrived back at the park gates. "Now all my poppies and lovely red flowers will bloom beautifully again," she went on. "I must take my precious petal back to Fairyland where it belongs."

She waved her wand over the petal, and it immediately shrank back to its Fairyland size. Pippa took the petal from Kirsty's hand and smiled. "Goodbye, girls," she cried, "and good luck with finding the other petals."

Rachel and Kirsty waved as Pippa disappeared in a burst of poppy-red sparkles.

"Another magic petal found," Kirsty said happily. "Now we'd better get back to Blossom Hall!"

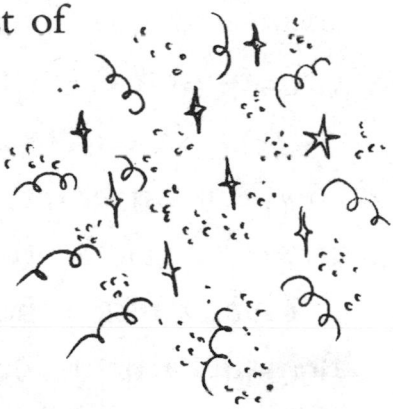

"Ooh, let's collect our flowers from the shop first!" Rachel reminded her.

The girls cycled back to Petal Perfection.

Kate was looking much happier when they walked in. "Hello again, girls," she called cheerfully. "Look at my flowers. Some of them have perked up no end since you were here before."

Kirsty and Rachel could see that all the poppies and the red flowers were now looking bright and healthy. They grinned at each other.

"Pippa's magic petal is working again already!" Kirsty whispered.

"Tell me which flowers you'd like," said Kate. "You've got more to choose from now."

The girls chose red and orange poppies, and Kate made them up into two pretty posies. Then Rachel and Kirsty said goodbye and cycled back to Blossom Hall.

"Look, Rachel," said Kirsty, "all the poppies in the hedgerows are blooming again!"

"Don't they look beautiful?" Rachel agreed happily, looking at the silky crimson heads nodding in the warm breeze. "I'm so glad we helped another Petal Fairy today."

The Petal Fairies

Pippa the Poppy Fairy has got her magic petal back. Now Rachel and Kirsty must help

Louise the Lily Fairy